SECRET
MESSAGE

A STORY WITH HIDDEN CLUES
FROM THE PAST -
TO MARK THE CENTENARY OF
WORLD WAR ONE

Leeds City College
Withdrawn From Stock

In Flanders fields the poppies blow
Between the crosses, row on row,
That mark our place; and in the sky
The larks, still bravely singing, fly
Scarce heard amid the guns below.

John McCrae

If any question why we died
Tell them that our fathers lied.

Rudyard Kipling

3

The Secret Message
by John Townsend

Published by Ransom Publishing Ltd.
Radley House, 8 St. Cross Road, Winchester, Hampshire SO23 9HX, UK
www.ransom.co.uk

ISBN   978 178127 275 6
First published in 2013

THE SECRET MESSAGE

John Townsend

RANS⬤M

Lying deceives. Hiding the truth destroys.

CONTENTS

The difference between a lie and a story is that a lie tries to hide the truth while a story tries to find it.

THE CLICK OF A MOUSE

I never knew it was there. Every night the secret was just above my head, in the darkness. I had no idea ... never in my wildest dreams. Then something struck in the middle of the night that changed everything.

Since we moved house three years ago when I was eight, I didn't have a clue what was up in the loft. But a mystery that no one had discovered before was just over my bedroom. It was me who eventually found it. It was me who finally worked out the clues, cracked the code and solved the riddle. It was me who uncovered the incredible truth from 100 years ago. It was me who first saw what it all means. You could say it was like double vision. You'll soon see why.

The question I'm dying to answer now is very simple. Could anyone else work it out and unlock the secret message? Can you? I'll tell the whole story and you can see for yourself. You might be able to puzzle it out faster than I did – if you can spot the signs. Keep a close lookout for the clues as I tell you the story that stunned my dad, made my mum cry and changed me forever.

I was woken in the middle of the night. A sudden clattering noise filled my room for just a few seconds. I sat up, blinking into total darkness.

After a final click and clunk above my ceiling there was only silence ... so I flopped back to sleep.

I forgot all about that noise in the night until next morning, when my little brother Ben blurted, 'Oh by the way, Mum – someone was up in the roof last night. They were walking around in the loft.'

We all stared at Ben as if he was mad, but then it all came back to me. So I said, 'Yeah, I remember now – something woke me in the night.'

'In that case, Sam,' Dad winked, 'You can come with me to investigate. But be warned ... we might find a dead body.' He paused for dramatic effect before adding with a smile, 'I set mousetraps up there a few days ago. Do you still want to climb the ladder into that mousey world of creepy cobwebs?'

I'd only been in the loft once, but I loved it up

there. It wasn't scary, just full of dusty clutter, dark shapes and boxes covered with curtains. It had strange smells and little piles of chewed cardboard left by mice. It would be a great place for a den. I followed my dad up the ladder and poked my head into the cold, eerie world above our bedrooms. I had to be careful where I trod, because Dad said I mustn't poke my foot through to the bathroom.

A mousetrap above my bedroom had snapped shut and the cheese had gone. The mouse that woke me in the night had a lucky escape. I lifted a sheet beside another trap and uncovered a stack of cases. It was there I saw a small, brown leather case that looked very old and unusual.

'What's this?' I asked Dad.

'That belonged to your great great grandfather. Do you remember my Grandad Peter? He left me that case, which was his father's. I've never looked inside as it's locked and I don't have the key.

Apparently it's got stuff about the First World War in it, so I don't think it will interest you.'

'Can I bring it down so we can have a look?' I asked. 'We're learning a bit about the war at school.'

He let me carry the little case downstairs where he looked at it carefully.

'I'm afraid I'll have to get some tools on this so we can open it up,' Dad said.

He then went to a drawer and, after a lot of searching, he found an old photograph and put it in my hand. 'This was the owner of that case. Meet your great great grandad. You're in for a shock, Sam.'

I stared at the face of a boy standing in a cornfield. He was dressed very smartly in an old-fashioned school uniform with an unusual collar. On the back of the photo there was faded writing in pencil: *GH 1911*. But it was the boy's face I couldn't stop staring at. It was just like I was looking in a mirror. If I hadn't known otherwise, I would have sworn it was me.

SEEING DOUBLE

If you ask me, all babies look alike. I don't know why grown-ups go on and on about which relatives a new baby looks like most. When my little sister was born, Dad and I laughed every time someone said, 'Oh, doesn't she look just like Ems when she was a baby?' Ems is my mum and she told me it was just the same when I was born – when old aunties kept saying, 'Oh, doesn't Sam look just like his great great grandad? He's the spitting image – an exact double.'

I've grown up knowing that long ago a man I never knew looked just like me. I'd seen some of the crumpled brown photos in a box in Dad's desk, but I hadn't seen the one of the boy in the field before. I have to agree that we do look so alike. I think it's our eyes and the shape of our chin.

My younger twin brothers, Ben and Tom, look nothing like me. They just look like each other! Twins, so they say, run in our family (Dad says noses do, too!) so I've always felt a bit left out by not being a twin myself. But I think it's really cool to have a sort of twin from the past, even though he died long ago and we never met. He's made me feel a bit special sometimes ... but nothing like as extraordinary as when I saw that photo. It was the moment I knew I had to find out more about my twin from 100 years ago.

My dad gave me a little frame to put the photo in. He said, 'You can hang it on your bedroom wall with your drawings.' So that's what I did. I put it between my two favourite paintings. One is a flying skylark which I drew from a book and then added a tree and a field in the background. The other is a close-up of a poppy I picked from a ditch. I thought it looked so lonely with its bent stalk, so I put it in a jar and painted it in watercolours. Everyone said what a good job I'd done, so I'm really proud of those two pictures. But now I have a third to look at every night before I go to sleep. It's my twin in a suit with a strange collar.

I was drawing at the kitchen table when Dad came in with that case I'd found. He said, 'I'm afraid I've had to mangle it up to get it open, but at least you can now look at what's in it. Nothing much!'

The case was lined with smooth red silk and

there were just two books inside. One was a small black Bible and the other had a burgundy leather cover.

'It looks as if your great great grandad typed up his memoirs and stuck them on the pages in that book. I haven't read them yet, so maybe you'd like to take first peep, Sam.' Dad then put another battered little case on the table, which he unzipped to show an old portable typewriter inside. 'I remember my grandad telling me this belonged to his father as well. It must have been used to type those pages.'

I gently placed my fingers on the typewriter keys. It felt really weird to be touching something that my twin had once touched. It was also weird that four of the keys had blobs of hard wax stuck on them. 'Why are those letters blotted out?' I asked.

Dad shook his head. 'No idea. Maybe he didn't like … ' he paused to work out which keys were covered, ' ... 6, Y, H and N. Maybe hot wax spilled over the typewriter and set on those particular keys. Anyway – have a little read and let me know if you find anything interesting in that leather book. Don't expect anything too exciting!'

Little did my dad know what I was about to discover. When I went to bed that night, I opened the book and slowly began to read the first page. Like all the pages, it had a typed sheet of thin paper stuck on it. A few inside were upside down. I must have been the first person for ages to read these forgotten words that were older than my dad. Maybe no one alive knew what story they told.

I so wanted to find out about the man who was my double – or maybe I'm *his* double. So I plumped up the pillows on my bed, pulled the duvet up to my chin and began reading the faint words in front of me ...

OUR STORY

by Frederick Ovel

There is more to Freddy Ovel than meets the eye (and far more than meets his own eye).

On his 80th birthday (in 1980) it is time, at last, to tell the whole story.

The basic facts are these: Freddy was born in a little cottage in the heart of the countryside. It belonged to the Squire, as did much of the land for miles around. Freddy's father worked in the Squire's stables – not that Freddy ever knew Pa, who was killed by a carthorse in an accident shortly before Freddy was born.

The Squire let Mrs Ovel and her children (Freddy, brother Harry and sister Maud) stay on in the cottage, despite there being no breadwinner to pay the rent. Ma worked hard tending a plot of land to grow food for the family and to sell for a few pennies. But country children at that time, more often than not, had an absolute whale of a time. The glorious fields were a wonderland of adventure – and the hay meadow was a magical, summer playground. It was another world then.

Squire Hoadley and his bossy wife lived at *The Grange*, in beautiful grounds surrounded by tall hedges, up a long drive behind ornate iron gates that were always shut. Everyone said their only child, Giles Hoadley, was 'wrapped in cotton wool' and never allowed into the village. Much of the time he lived away at boarding school and never set eyes on other children in the village. Giles had a privileged childhood in so many ways, yet he was starved of the most important thing of all – a loving family. Freddy, on the other hand, had the happiest of families, despite all their hardships. These two boys, like flip-sides of a coin, grew up less than a mile apart yet without ever meeting – for all intents and purposes ... at least, to begin with.

In the cottage next to the Ovels lived another family, with two children; Daisy and Gordon. Both families shared a pig that they fattened on scraps all year, till the day the pig man called. After the killing and butchering, the two families had half each to salt and hang up for ham and bacon through the winter.

Daisy from next door was best friends with Maud and Harry, while Freddy looked after her brother. Some people in the village called Gordon a simpleton. In fact, he'd had a head injury as a baby. At the village cricket match a ball flew to the boundary and smashed into his pram. He was lucky to survive but his abilities were impaired, which made most children laugh at him ... but never Freddy – who cared for him like a brother.

It was in the summer of 1911 when Freddy's life changed. One evening, as the children ran through the hay meadow, Freddy happened to look across the valley into the Squire's orchard, lit magically by a crimson setting sun.

'Hey, look at all them bright red cherries in the trees,' he panted. 'How about picking a few?'

Maud cuffed him round the head. 'Don't you dare think about such things, Freddy Ovel. Ma would skin you alive if she ever found out. It isn't just stealing. You know what she says about you going anywhere near the Squire's land.'

Harry joined in. 'Maud and me can go in the Squire's wood, but you're strictly forbidden, Freddy. Ma says you're the baby of the family and must stay close to home. She lost Pa on the Squire's estate, so she says she can't risk her youngest going there.'

Gordon looked up and said slowly, 'Is the Squire a bad man, then?'

'No, Gordon,' Freddy answered calmly, 'The Squire's been very good to let us stay in his cottage, as we can't afford to pay the rent. He's usually quick to turf people out, but Ma says we've been "mercifully spared".'

Daisy grabbed Gordon by the hand and ran

to the top of the hill, with Maud and Harry in hot pursuit. Freddy stood where he was and stared across at the orchard. The cherry-pickers had gone and their ladders were still propped against the trees ... waiting.

'I love cherries,' Freddy whispered. He looked all around, but the others had disappeared over the brow of the hill. It was now or never ... so he darted back down the valley, leapt over the brook and clambered the fence into the orchard. He was soon up in the branches, laden with the plumpest of ripe fruit. Just as he crammed yet another handful of cherries into his mouth, he heard a voice below.

'Are you one of Papa's cherry pickers by any chance?'

Almost falling out of the tree, Freddy quickly wiped the juice from his mouth and dropped to the ground, twisting his ankle as he landed with a thud. Despite the pain and a cherry stone in his throat, he tried to speak as calmly as he could manage.

'I'm exploring, that's all. Just admiring the view. Hope you don't mind.' He began choking as he looked up to see a pair of eyes staring back at him. Deep blue eyes just like his own ... from a face exactly like his – but without the scratches. The boy staring at him in disbelief was the same height and build, but he wore a tweed suit with buttoned waistcoat and Eton collar.

'How extraordinary,' the boy said. 'Whoever are you?'

'I'm Freddy. Freddy Ovel from just down the brook. I've never seen you round here before.'

The boy held a sketchpad and pencil. 'Remarkable. Not that I live here much. I've only just returned from boarding school.'

'Is your pa the Squire?'

'That's right. I've come down here to

sketch. Are you all right? You seem to be making a strange face.'

Freddy tried to stop wincing. 'It's my ankle, that's all – but if my face is strange, so is yours! You look just like ... '

'Yes, I know. It's absurd. Listen, I think I need to tell you something ... '

Freddy knew he could get in big trouble. He'd been caught red-handed by the Squire's own son. He tried to change the subject. 'I like drawing, too. Can I see your sketch?'

The boy held out his pad. 'Of course. This is only a line drawing, but I may paint it later. My nanny showed me how to do different types of shading – do you see?'

Freddy was impressed. 'That's so clever. I wish I could draw like that. Er ... how old are you?'

The boy tucked the drawing under his arm and carefully placed the pencil in his breast pocket. 'I shall be twelve in January.'

Freddy gasped. 'It wouldn't be the seventeenth, would it?'

'However did you know? Have you got psychic powers?' He stared at Freddy in stunned silence before leaning forward and peering directly into his eyes. 'Would you mind if I just look at your eyes really closely?' They stood nose to nose. 'How peculiar! How tall are you?'

Freddy shrugged as the boy announced, 'I suggest we stand back to back and compare heights. We seem to be like two peas in a pod.' His hand rested on the top of both their heads. 'Put your hand against mine. That's amazing. We're completely identical. I'm Giles, by the way. But listen, I've got to tell you something about the cherries ... '

Freddy felt himself blushing. 'Sorry. You're not going to tell anyone are you? I only ate a few.'

'I thought as much. In that case, you ought to know the truth. For some reason, most of those cherries are full of maggots.'

Whether it was the effect of what he heard, the shooting pain in his ankle or the shock of meeting his double, Freddy was violently sick ... before he passed out.

It was the smell of horses that dragged him back. Freddy opened his eyes and blinked up at a wooden roof and straw bales stacked in a tottering pile. He heard a horse snorting close by and the distant trilling of a skylark. Then he felt the warm, syrupy cherry-sick sticking to his shirt and the burning in his throat. As the cramps in his stomach returned, he began retching again.

'Here he is. This is the boy. I managed to get him into the stable, but I think he needs a doctor.' Giles stood over him anxiously, as the

Squire's housekeeper bustled in with a bucket and cloth. 'Do you think he's going to live, Miss Greet?'

She stooped to wipe Freddy's face, but when she saw it, she froze. He looked up at her and groaned. 'I'm sorry. I'm never going to eat another cherry as long as I live.'

'Oh glory! Cherries are the least of our worries,' Miss Greet mumbled, propping him against a bale before adding, 'You shouldn't have fetched me, Master Giles.'

'I couldn't ask Mama as she doesn't like to get her hands grubby, and she won't let me talk to the villagers.'

Miss Greet responded curtly, 'You were right not to tell her. She must never know.'

Giles stepped back as Freddy was sick again. 'I think he must have eaten a lot of cherries.'

She wiped her hands on her apron and

sighed. 'I'm not bothered right now about wretched cherries. And I suggest you forget about them, too. I've got serious thinking to do. I always knew it was wrong to split twins up like that.'

Freddy pulled himself up and repeated feebly, 'Twins?'

She hesitated before gabbling on without taking a breath, 'This has really let the cat out the bag. I'll get shot if they find out. But I suppose it's only right you hear the truth, now that you've met. I always knew it was bound to happen. But you must both promise me never to say anything. Will you promise to keep this a secret and never tell a soul?' They both nodded, looking completely confused.

'In that case,' she went on, 'this is the gist of it ... and to think it's in here where it happened shortly before you were born. It was only my second week of working for the

Squire as housekeeper when the accident happened. This was where your poor father met his end. A terrible accident. I fetched the doctor but it was too late.'

Freddy sat up on the bale. 'Ma's told me about how Pa died and how our cottage came with his job. She says we've been very fortunate to be allowed to stay on without having to pay rent to the Squire.'

Giles was still frowning as Miss Greet continued in a secretive whisper. 'Your poor mother, Freddy. She was in a terrible state. She could hardly afford to feed her older children, let alone the third due. When it turned out to be twin boys, you can imagine her anguish. Not that she didn't want to keep both, of course. But she knew you'd all end up in the workhouse and her children would doubtless be taken away.'

Giles spoke for the first time. 'That's

terrible. So what about ... I mean, what about my Mama?'

'She couldn't have children of her own, and the Squire was desperate for a son and heir to carry on the Hoadley name. The agreement was that he would let your ma stay on in the cottage if they could raise one of her babies as theirs. But the deal was that no one must ever know, or she'd have to move away. And that would mean the workhouse – so she had to agree never to set eyes on her adopted son and never to speak of him again.'

Giles sat beside Freddy on the bale in total disbelief. 'Me. So I was the one to come and live here?'

'That's right,' she went on, looking over her shoulder as if the horses were listening to every forbidden word. 'But I've been sworn to secrecy and it's more than my job's worth. It's just that when I saw you together just now, it seemed ... No, I should have kept my mouth shut. Forgive me for telling.'

Giles turned to look at Freddy directly. 'It's all a bit of a shock, actually. I woke up this morning an only child, and now I've got a brother. And he looks like ... that!'

Freddy smiled for the first time. 'Two brothers, actually. Harry's a couple of years older. And a sister. Maud's a year older than us. You'll have to come and meet them.'

Miss Greet shouted, startling one of the horses. 'No! That you can't do. Never. I wish I hadn't spilled the beans now. I reckon I've well and truly upset the applecart.'

After a long pause, Giles stood and said thoughtfully, 'I'm glad you've told us, Miss Greet. It just takes some getting used to, that's all. Don't you think so, Freddy? We can still see each other. We can meet in secret. I'd like that.'

The colour was returning to Freddy's cheeks as he stood to look Giles in the face. 'I won't tell a living soul. Besides, if I say anything to Ma, she'll box my ears for coming on the Squire's land.'

'In that case,' Giles said, offering his hand, 'we'd better shake. As a pact. We'll swear an oath to be loyal to each other and always keep our friendship a secret. We must never tell anyone without each other's permission.'

They shook hands firmly and their promise was sealed. Forever.

Secret Meetings

Freddy and Giles became the closest of friends
– growing up together and sharing their
deepest thoughts whenever school holidays
allowed. Their meetings were often at night in
the stables or in the hay meadow at dawn
where they played, chatted endlessly and
watched the soaring skylarks in the clouds.

They sent each other coded letters, left in a

secret gap behind a plank in the stable. It was
Giles who came up with the code to use.

'Seeing as you're mad about skylarks, why
don't we learn these lines from a poem called
The Skylark?' He showed Freddy a page from
a poetry book:

Opening their golden caskets to the sun,
The buttercups make schoolboys eager run,
To see who shall be first to pluck the prize –
Up from their hurry, see, the skylark flies

'All we have to do is number the lines and
letters, and we can make secret messages that
no one else will understand if they find them.
So long as we don't need the letters J, Q, V, X
and Z we'll be fine. So, to write the word *Freddy*
all I have to do is find an F, which is in line 4
and the third letter. So F is 4:3. Your whole
name will be: **4:3**, **4:4**, **1:3**, **1:16**, **1:16**, **4:16**.

'What do you think?'

Freddy leapt up excitedly. 'It's like our own special, secret magic!'

Their coded letters and covert meetings stopped during term time – but the holidays became their happiest times of all. When Giles's Mama discovered one of Freddy's coded notes in the parlour, she insisted Giles explained to her what it meant.

'Just some numbers, Mama. It's a sort of puzzle I'm inventing, that's all.'

Her icy stare convinced him she didn't believe him. 'You should never spend time on such nonsense. You must study your Latin and Greek, so go to your room immediately.'

Christmas 1913 brought few meetings, as deep snow threatened to reveal their footprints across the stable yard. With Freddy and

Gordon now working at a dairy in the next village (his mother wouldn't let him ask the Squire for a job), there were fewer chances to meet up. So, just before Giles was due to return to school, they braved a blizzard to meet at midnight in one of the outbuildings. Clutching lanterns and gifts, they huddled in the straw while icy wind rattled the bolted door.

'These presents are for Christmas, but also our fourteenth birthday,' Giles began. Freddy looked embarrassed. 'I'm afraid I haven't got any money for proper presents, so I've got you these. I hope you like them.'

Giles tore off the tissue paper to reveal two pictures and a little wooden carved dog.

'That's my most precious thing in the world,' Freddy said. 'But I want you to have it. Our Pa made it and Ma wanted me to have it – but I've enjoyed it for fourteen years, so now

41

it's your turn for the next fourteen. You can give it back then!'

Giles was speechless as he turned the little carving around in his fingers. 'Thank you so much, Freddy. I will treasure this. And this little painting of a bird – it's perfect. You can draw and paint much better than me. Just look at this lovely brush work and the way you've coloured the feathers so delicately. And this flower looks so real ... '

Freddy grinned proudly. 'I'm glad you like it. I made the brushes. The cat's missing a few chunks off his tail! I also made the colour washes myself from soil and plants.'

'Freddy, you're so clever.' Giles fell silent for a long time before adding, 'Your life is so much richer than mine. I've got nothing. Just my inheritance one day. But that means nothing. You're everything to me now. You and your family.'

'*OUR* family. So what did your Mama and Papa give you for Christmas?'

Giles looked away. 'Actually, they don't give me presents. They never have. But here, have a look at yours.' He handed Freddy a small box tied with a purple ribbon. As he untied it and opened the lid, Freddy gasped and took out a watch on a chain.

'No, Giles, you can't give me this. It's the most valuable thing I've ever seen.'

Just then another gust of snowy wind tore at the door, stirred the straw around their feet and flickered their lanterns. They dived behind a pile of sacks in panic ... only to laugh helplessly when they discovered it was just the wind. That night, despite the biting cold, they each realised their friendship was warmer and deeper than ever before. Neither of them imagined it could ever end. But next Christmas the world would be very different.

THE GREAT WAR

Everyone was talking about the war long
before its ripples began to reach the village.

A few of the Squire's workers joined up and
went off to fight somewhere across the
Channel. They and the soldiers rounding up
farm horses to take off to France all boasted of
giving the Hun a bloody nose – and all would
be over by Christmas. But it wasn't.

In fact, just before Christmas, the newspapers reported that British towns on the east coast were fired on by German ships. Over one hundred people, including children, were killed in one attack. The enemy was despised more than ever.

The following year, Zeppelins began bombing Britain. These German airships killed civilians, caused destruction and brought blackouts to London. More young men rushed to join up, all keen to do their patriotic duty. In 1916, Harry Ovel was almost old enough to enlist as a soldier so, after a little white lie, he proudly went off to France in his smart new uniform. Maud waved him off, cheering and singing while his mother wept into her hanky.

By the end of the year, Harry's letters home no longer shone with his usual sparkle and wit. Even so, Freddy read every word carefully and showed the letters to Giles.

'I can't wait till I can go out there and join Harry,' Freddy said. 'I'm dying to do my bit for King and Country. Not only that, I'd get to travel and see other countries. I'm not like you, Giles – I've never been more than a few miles from home. I need to *LIVE*.'

In the Easter holidays of 1917, the twins met in the stable – for that conversation they'd been waiting for. It was Giles who started it.

'Freddy, what do you think I should do? My headmaster says I should go up to Oxford next year to study Classics. He's teaching me Latin and says I'd make a good scholar and an officer. But I just don't think that's for me. I can't talk to Mama or Papa because they want me to become a businessman and run this place. I'd hate that, too.'

Freddy laughed. 'You're lucky to have a

choice! Gordon and me struggle on at the dairy, where I have to keep a close eye on him. But he's a good sort and … ' he paused to watch for a reaction. 'I promised Daisy I'd look after him. You see, Daisy and me are now er … '

'Sweethearts, is that it?'

'Yeah. I'd like you to meet her, Giles. She's lovely. She's now working as a parlour maid for the rector. But listen, I've been thinking. When Harry comes home on leave, why don't we plan a big surprise? You can come and see Daisy, Maud and Ma. I'll warn her first.'

Giles beamed. 'I've always wanted to see them all. I can't wait. I just don't want to upset Ma, that's all.'

'Talking of upsetting people,' Freddy fidgeted awkwardly, 'I don't know what you'll think about what I'm going to say. I know some twins can tell what the other is thinking but … '

Giles held Freddy's arm. 'I know exactly what you're thinking. I've been thinking it too. I want to come with you. We could join up together. We'd have to lie about our age, but it would be wonderful to be together and away from all this.'

Freddy paced up and down, excited and yet unsure. 'You read my mind exactly, but I had no idea you'd want to come as well. Harry said half the boys who enlisted with him were under nineteen and lied. Some were as young as fifteen. They all do it and the army turns a blind eye. Our country needs us all. The thing is, I just have to convince Ma and Daisy. But I will. Giles, we'll do it. We'll go. We'll fight the Hun side by side and end this war once and for all.'

Freddy patiently explained to Gordon all about Giles as the three of them walked across the market square in town at the Easter Fair. Despite being told many times, Gordon was still confused. 'But I can't tell which of you is which.'

Freddy grinned. 'This is the only difference.' He pulled his shirt collar down over his left shoulder, to reveal a small red mark. 'I've got a birthmark but Giles hasn't! It's a bit like an upside-down letter **f** for Freddy.'

'That's no good to me,' Gordon smiled. 'I can't read.'

Suddenly a commanding cry rang out from the steps of the town hall, which was draped in flapping Union Jack bunting. A sergeant major barked orders at a military band marching past, where sunlight danced from a swirl of glinting brass. A crowd gathered and clapped at the impressive walrus-moustached figure on the steps.

'Ladies and gentlemen, I'm not going to mince my words. To be perfectly frank, we're taking a right bashing over the Channel. Our chaps are putting on a jolly good show, but it only needs a few spanners in the works for things to go skew-whiff. To put it bluntly, it's a darn sweat. In short, this old war is turning out to be a bit of a tough nut to crack. We need fresh blood out there to help chivvy our boys. So who's prepared to come with me and give the Bosch a damned good hiding?

'My question is simple: Do you want to wake up with the Hun in your bed? Well, do you? Do you? DO YOU?' He pointed directly at Gordon and all heads turned.

Gordon hesitated and stuttered, 'I ain't got a bed. I sleep on the couch.'

As quick as a flash, the officer barked back. 'Then you need to join His Majesty's Army so you can sleep at night with a clear conscience and a true British sense of pride.'

No one was prepared for Gordon's response. 'Not me, sir. I'm a bit simple, sir.'

There was instant muttering from the crowd before the sergeant major retorted, 'You can hold a rifle, can't you? Then you're just who we need. Who'll be the first brave lad to come here and take the King's shilling? I'm looking for boys with hearts of oak – and we'll turn you into men of steel.'

A man in the crowd called out, 'Come on boys, what's keeping you? Why aren't your fathers telling you? All fathers here say "aye" if you agree these boys should go out there and all pull together. It'll be a piece of cake, won't it men?'

They all shouted 'Aye!'

Freddy rushed forward. 'I will. I want to join up, sir.' There were loud cheers.

'Splendid,' the officer smirked. 'And what

about your friends? Are they men of courage, or cowards? Will they be champions or chickens? Do they want medals blazoned on their chests, or white feathers stuffed in their lily-white palms?'

Giles ran to join Freddy at the recruiting desk. 'And me, I want to go with him.'

Many in the crowd looked with disbelief as if they were seeing double. Gordon stepped forward gingerly and called up to the sergeant major. 'In that case, I don't suppose you've got room for one more?'

THE TRENCHES

After training camp, the new recruits were kitted up and soon sailing across the Channel. Men, horses, artillery and supplies landed in France under leaden skies, before the convoy headed eastwards towards Flanders, through driving rain over rutted roads grey with mud.

Daisy and Ma anxiously waited for news, while the Squire and his wife were furious.

After Sunday Evensong, Squire Hoadley made a public announcement in church that he disowned his wretched son for leaving no more than a scribbled note declaring he had abandoned his education to enlist while under age. 'These are the thanks we get as devoted parents. Our son sneaks off to become no more than a rookie private, when he should be top officer class. It's an utter disgrace.'

As soon as they got to their sleeping quarters close to the front, the new recruits met their sergeant, who clearly intended to make their lives a misery.

'You lot are in for a treat, I can tell you. Heaven help you if you fail to obey your superiors at all times. That's me. When I say "jump", you leap ... or else.'

He looked directly at Freddy and Giles. 'And

what have we got here, then? Tweedle Dum and Tweedle Dee. Name?'

'Private Ovel, sir.'

'Two Ovels, I see.'

'No, sir,' Giles corrected him. 'I'm Private Hoadley.'

The sergeant pressed his nose up against Giles's and barked, 'Rule one: Never tell me I'm wrong, lad. I smell a rat. If I say yer twins, don't answer back. Just because you try to sound all lah-di-dah, Hoadley – it don't mean you can impress me, you little jumped-up maggot. Do you take me for a fool?'

Giles was about to respond, but Freddy stopped him. 'One of us was adopted, sir.'

The sergeant paused and sneered. 'Is that so? I can tell you're the dregs of the two, Ovel. Listen all of you. I'm telling you where you'll be working first; shoring-up and tunnelling. "C" section is laying explosives, so they'll need their kip when they come back shortly. That means quiet. Then you lot take over. Do I make myself clear?'

'Yessir.' Gordon's swift response surprised them all. He smiled proudly and gave Freddy a wink.

'And another thing ... ' the sergeant sneered. 'When you write home, I'll be reading every word and tearing up anything that gives away information or tells things as they really are – such as you're soaking wet all day and night, you're itching with lice, swarming with rats or you've got the runs and foot rot. Is that clear, Private Hoadley?'

'Yes sir.'

As the weeks passed, the sergeant's taunts never stopped. If any letters came through from home, Giles received nothing. He had no one to write to, either. The sergeant jibed him constantly as 'Lonely Hoadley'.

Freddy would read Gordon's letters to him. Daisy wrote regularly to them both, but Freddy would sit for long periods alone whenever he heard from her. Giles could tell he was troubled, but then the day came when a letter arrived that reduced Freddy to tears. The news finally reached him that brother Harry had been killed a month ago at Ypres. Giles tried to console him, but that night they both wept together as never before.

Autumn arrived with more rain, heavy mists and freezing nights. The back-breaking work of digging tunnels and building trenches continued with little rest. Only when shells were falling or there were threats of gas attacks could work be stopped.

It was while they were resting and playing cards one evening that the sergeant burst in.

'Stand by your beds. We've just received orders from HQ. I need a patrol immediately. Grab your rifles at the double. We're to find out what size regiments have come into the line opposite – however far that might be. Maps are still patchy, and due to fog and failing light, spotter planes haven't got that information. Our orders are to go on foot now – while visibility's poor and we're out of sight. Instructions are to creep up on enemy lines, grab a prisoner and bring him back for interrogation. Get your gasmasks and over we go. Hurry up, you lot, move yourselves ... '

No Man's Land

The night was thick with smoke and clinging fog. As they clambered from the dugout through oozing clay and twisted wire, the heavy blanket of mist engulfed them. Stumbling with heads down through soupy, putrid puddles, they couldn't see a thing – not even each other. Freddy looked up to see if any lights on the horizon might give a sense of direction – as a hand grabbed his shoulder and pulled him into the mud.

'Keep your head down, you imbecile,' the sergeant hissed. 'Don't move a muscle. That's an order. This blasted fog is thicker than they warned and these binoculars are useless. I reckon it's that way.' He pointed to the left.

'But if I'm not mistaken, sir ... ' Giles interrupted, 'the German lines were due north and we now seem to be heading west into the minefield.'

The sergeant swore and swung round with eyes raging. 'Who the hell told you to speak? You're a private, so what do you know? Just because you're posh, you know better, eh? Then let me tell you, sunshine – we're in the middle of ruddy no-man's land, that's where we are.'

A sudden blast threw a spray of mud and a plume of acrid smoke over their sprawling bodies. Gordon whimpered and the sergeant snapped, 'Shut your whinging, lad. Get up and follow me.'

Freddy couldn't stop himself. 'I think my brother was right, sir. Shouldn't we get our bearings first?'

The sergeant spat back. 'You're an idiot, Ovel. I give the orders round here. When I say we go, we go in the direction I command. Got it? I've already decided the Hun's position. Here's the proof. Ovel, raise your rifle above your head.'

Freddy stared in dismay. 'Sir?'

'I said hold up your rifle. If Fritz doesn't fire, we know it's safe to make a run for it.'

'And if they do fire, sir?'

'I reassess. Don't worry, lad – they won't hit from this distance. Not in this fog.'

Freddy knew the risk of answering back, but he couldn't stop himself. 'What distance?

We don't know where we are, sir.'

'Raise your rifle, Ovel. That's an order. Hold your rifle above your head for five seconds.'

Giles couldn't bear to watch. 'Freddy, I don't think you should ... '

The obscenity flew louder than a gunshot. 'Are you questioning my order? That's a court martial offence. I'll have you done for cowardice if you dare speak again.'

Scrambling to his knees, Freddy gabbled desperately, 'All right, sir. I'll do it. Here goes ... '

He gingerly lifted his rifle above his head, as the sergeant counted slowly.

'You see, lad – what's all the fuss? Fritz can't see a thing either.'

A sudden shot ripped past them. Freddy fell back into a crater, tangled in razor wire.

Giles slithered through the mud to reach him, as the sergeant barked, 'He's not hit, you fool. My plan worked. Now we know where they are, we make a dash for it in the opposite direction – to the right.' He paused before he sputtered, 'I can smell gas – get out of here. On your feet, damn you.'

Giles was holding Freddy's grazed head out of the mud. 'What about Freddy? I've got to cut him free.'

'Leave him. It's too risky. I'll send a rescue later when it's safe. He'll have to take his chance. Leave him there. That's an order. Follow me.'

The other soldiers scuttled after him through the smoke, as Giles called, 'I'm not leaving him, sir. If mustard gas gets him, he's done for. He'll need help with his gasmask.'

The sergeant spun back and grabbed him by the throat. 'Are you disobeying an order, boy? You'll get mown down by machine guns and grenades.'

'I'm just telling you, sergeant. He's my brother. He cracked his head and he's unconscious. I must stay with him. Never mind about me, sir. Go back without me. I'll carry him back when it's safe. Sir.'

The hand at his throat tightened. 'I don't care if he's the Queen of bloody Sheba, you'll do as I command without question, you half-wit. Get up. You're coming with me.'

'He's my BROTHER!' Giles pushed the man off him with a forceful shove, sending him sprawling in the mud, then turned back to Freddy, who lay face-down with his eyes still shut. 'It's all right; I won't leave you, Freddy. Wake up, you're going to be all right. I promise.'

The sergeant staggered to his feet and growled, 'It'll be far better for you to get gassed than face the music for striking an officer.' He swore again and disappeared into the fog.

Frantically trying to wake Freddy, while struggling to pull on both their gasmasks, Giles was already choking from the burning in his throat and churning fear in the pit of his stomach. He lay beside Freddy in cold silence as yellow sulphurous smoke rolled towards them. After what seemed an eternity, he raised his head to peer into the night ... when a blinding flash burst just in front of him and tore away his mask. He fell back screaming, as if white-hot splinters were burning into his eyes. 'I can't see. Freddy, I can't see!'

They held each other in the darkness as the choking stench slowly seeped away and the deadly cloud drifted over. They continued clinging to one another through the night, gasping, groaning, whispering and praying in their sodden, stinking hell.

At long last, as the sky began to lighten in the east, a silver mist hung above their heads in the deathly stillness. Freddy stirred. 'I think I heard a skylark. Over there. The larks are in the fields behind our trenches. It's the way back.'

Numb with cold, they slowly wriggled free from the wire and stagnant mud sucking them down, to emerge from their boggy crater. Giles could only murmur deliriously as they propped each other up and limped back through the reeking quagmire. Freddy steadily steered him past gruesome shapes in the mud – the twisted limbs of corpses. Giles saw nothing. He could no longer see anything … and never would again.

THE WAIT

They sat in the medical tent, wrapped in blankets and sipping strong, sweet tea. Freddy's torn arm was put in a sling and he was led back to camp with a curt, 'Nothing much wrong with you, Ovel.'

A medical officer wound a bandage around Giles's head, completely covering his eyes. 'You'll have to keep this on for a week. If your eyes are affected by exposure to mustard gas, your sight should return soon. If you need further treatment, I don't think there's much point bothering under the circumstances. I've been instructed to read you this letter then escort you to the cells.' He took a document from an envelope and slowly read aloud:

'Private 2634 Giles George Hoadley, the charge against you is that on the 19th October 1917, you did wilfully disobey orders from a superior officer and strike him, with the express intention of deserting your duty and subjecting both officer and fellow soldiers to increased danger. Such a wanton display of insubordination and cowardice carries the maximum penalty. The evidence will be examined and the sentence announced within twenty-eight days – delivered to your prison cell.'

For the endless days that followed, Giles was kept in total isolation in a small room with only a straw mattress and a bucket. Whether the cell had a window, he had no idea for he could see nothing. Apart from calling to the guard outside the door, he had no way of knowing the time of day or night. Then, without warning, he was led to a nearby room for questioning, but he had no idea how many men were there or who they were. It turned out to be the briefest of trials.

After long weeks of nothingness, waiting in fear and dread, the final verdict arrived. The guard was instructed to read it to the prisoner slowly.

'Having considered the evidence against you most thoroughly and having interviewed the respected officer whom you so wantonly disobeyed and struck in cowardice in front of fellow servicemen, Field Marshall Sir Charles Quinn has no alternative than to impose the maximum sentence. As an example to others that defiance on the field of battle can never be tolerated, Private 2634 Giles George Hoadley shall be executed by firing squad at 0700 hours on 11th November 1917.'

The guard paused before adding, 'I'm sorry.'

Giles didn't move. 'Not as much as I am. But I'm not surprised. I was born unlucky.'

After a long silence he spoke again. 'Are you still there? How long have I got?'

'Till tomorrow. You're allowed a visit if you wish.'

He gave a sigh. 'It's too late for a priest now.'

'I meant your brother. He's been waiting outside ... with a friend.'

Giles sat up on his bed. 'Really? I'd like to talk to them.'

The guard deliberated. 'I'll have to get permission for both. You'll have to wait.'

'I'm used to it. Will you show them that verdict? I may not be able to tell them myself.'

Hours later, a key rattled in the door and it clanged open. Giles heard footsteps and the guard whispering; 'Only five minutes. Orders. I have to be present.'

Freddy put his hands on Giles's shoulders. 'I've heard the news. I don't know what to say. You saved my life, Giles. Some of the men didn't make it back.'

Gordon was sobbing. 'We're really sorry.'

Giles reached out to him. 'I don't want tears. These minutes will be tough enough without tears. Who'd have thought it would come to this? It wasn't a proper trial. They'd already decided to make an example of me. I admitted to them what I did. We all knew it was a stupid order. They wouldn't let me have either of you for a witness as they said you're unreliable. They said Gordon was … '

'Simple?' Gordon croaked, 'But not too simple to be shot at.'

Giles continued, 'I asked for you, Freddy but they wouldn't let you because you're my brother. A brother with a different surname was considered an unreliable witness. I've always wanted a brother and then, in my hour of need, they wouldn't let you near me.'

Freddy fought back the tears. 'Giles, listen to me – and keep this in your heart till the end: You're the best friend I've ever had. The finest person I've ever known – with the greatest respect to you, Gordon. But Giles, I really mean it.'

Giles winced as tears stung his eyes. 'I know. But I'll tell you something, too. Freddy,

I've always wanted to be you. Just remember that. When all this is over and when you're back home in the hay meadows, never forget that I'll be there somewhere ... up there with the larks.'

They held each other, unable to speak. When Freddy squeezed Gordon's arm there followed a rasping of coughs and splutters. Freddy turned to the guard. 'Do you mind getting him some water? Please.'

The guard hesitated. 'Er ... But then your time will be up.' He left the room and locked the door as Freddy quickly pulled off his coat. 'Listen to me, Giles. I just want to give you a final gift. No arguments – I've given it careful thought. Make the most of it. I'm only sorry it might hurt at first.' He stood directly in front of him and raised his hand. 'I'm just glad you can't see what I've got to do. Goodbye, Giles and thanks for everything. Until we meet again ... ' The fist struck Giles full on the jaw and he fell back across the bed.

Freddy swiftly pulled the bandage off Giles's head and pushed it over his own.

'Hurry, Gordon. Give him the handkerchief and put my coat round his shoulders. Get him on his feet.'

Giles groaned as a key rattled in the lock. Gordon whimpered, 'Quick, he's coming.'

The guard entered with a cup of water to see Gordon still coughing and holding up the other visitor. It was the prisoner on the bed who spoke first. 'Thank you. My brother is too upset to say any more. I'd like them to go now. Goodbye, Gordon. Look after him for me. Have a good life, Freddy. Make the most of it. Oh Gordon ... give him back this watch. Tell him ... tell him our few years together were the best of my life.'

Holding the handkerchief to his eyes and

still stunned, Giles was helped from the room. Gordon supported him all the way back to their quarters, and then put him to bed.

With handkerchief tied over his eyes, Giles lay in a confused daze until morning. At seven o'clock he shuddered at a sudden rally of rifle shots somewhere in the distance. A chilling echo ripped through the freezing silence and he shrieked uncontrollably, as if a blade of ice had pierced his heart.

'Freddy left a note in your coat pocket,' Gordon said. 'I know you can't see it, so I'll try to read it to you. I'm really sorry, but it doesn't make sense. It's just a lot of numbers. I can't really do numbers.'

Giles asked him to read them aloud very slowly, each number at a time. It was a struggle, but at last Gordon managed to deliver Freddy's final message:

3:12, 1:1, 1:1, 1:22

2:15, 4:3, 2:1, 1:3, 2:9

1:16, 2:15, 1:5, 3:3, 4:16

2:15, 1:4, 1:16

1:1, 4:1, 2:9

2:4, 2:15, 2:4, 4:16

As well as being a good artist, Freddy wrote a few poems. Gordon found the last one in Freddy's kit bag. It was written the day before they killed him.

NOT HERE

Don't weep long after I have gone
But laugh and know that love lives on.
Don't trudge through sodden fields in
*   driving rain*
In some vain hope to meet again.
I won't be there.

Don't loiter in the cloistered must
In holy light through stained-glass dust,
To mourn on cold and silent pew
Reliving all the times we knew.
I won't be there.

Don't linger in each fingered sheet
Of scribbled words left incomplete,
Nor flick through faded photographs
Rekindling long-forgotten laughs.
I won't be there.

Don't wallow in the hollow void
Of empty dreams with hope destroyed,
Nor cling to trinkets left behind,
Or rotting wreaths round crumbling shrine.
I won't be there.

Don't think that on the brink of death
I didn't breathe my final breath

Without the strength and hope you gave ...
To be my shroud inside the grave.
But I'm not there.

For aren't I more than relics trapped,
Or memories tied, all neatly wrapped?
Like clasping hands round melting snow,
Or songbirds caged ... just let me go.
For I'm not here.

Like soaring larks, I'm flying free;
I'm part of you, as you of me.
And one day, when our pain is healed,
The sun will warm the poppy field ...
And maybe in a hundred years
A new beginning reappears ...
And I am there.
I shall be there.

Frederick Ovel (10th November, 1917)

Footnote

There is still an untold part to the story, but even now it is too difficult to tell here.

If someone wants to find the final piece of the jigsaw when I've gone and I'm safely out of this world – it is here:

N5, Y8, N5, H9, Y3

H3, Y3, Y7, Y5 29:29

H9, Y7, H8, Y3 8:17.

SAM'S DISCOVERY

I put down the book and snuggled under my duvet.
I think I must have stared at the ceiling for a long
time. Then I stared at my three pictures on the wall.
The story was so sad, and yet it didn't all make sense.

It wasn't difficult to work out the first coded
message. It used the same poem code as before.
But I just couldn't understand the other code in
the footnote.

I still had a big question and I was sure that footnote would answer it. Perhaps you've already guessed. I had to wait till morning before I could find out more.

I only told Dad some of what I'd read, and asked him if he knew when his great grandad died. 'I've no idea,' he answered. 'You'll have to ask Gran. We can Skype her if you like.'

Gran is my dad's mum and she lives miles away. I couldn't wait to talk to her.

As soon as her face appeared on the screen I said, 'Hi, Gran. Can I ask you about your grandad? Did you know him and when did he die?'

'Woah – all your questions, Sam! Yes Grandad lived very near us. In fact I used to guide him around town when I was a girl, before he got his guide dog. I know exactly when he died. It was in 1980, on the day before Daddy was born.'

I asked her if he ever spoke about the First World War to her.

'Not that I remember. I don't think he liked to, as it was when he lost his sight. It's amazing how he later managed living on his own and doing so many things.'

I held up his typewriter in front of the webcam. 'Do you recognise this?' I asked.

'Wow, I haven't seen that for years. I didn't know you had it! Grandad used that typewriter all the time. I learned to touch-type on it. The marked keys made it easier to learn. The wax on the middle keys helped him work out where all the letters were. He just had to count along from Y, H & N – or as he remembered them, *Your Home Number*. He did a lot of typing that way.'

'What about reading?' I asked. 'Did he use Braille?'

'He used a Braille watch and playing cards, but he found Moon a bit easier. That's another way of reading using touch. He read with his fingers from big books with raised shapes as letters. He sometimes borrowed a machine so he could type in Moon. It was very clever.'

By now my mind was whirring and I was really excited. I looked at the typewriter keys and started to see the code. N5 must mean the fifth letter on the N row, which is 'B'. Gran was going on about the alphabet games they used to play, but I wasn't really listening. I was too busy doing some alphabet work of my own. Suddenly the word 'Bible' jumped out at me and I knew I was on to something. But then Gran said something that made me look up.

'As children, Uncle John and I used to beg him to draw for us, as he'd once been a good artist. Even though he couldn't see, he drew lovely pictures for us with coloured chalks on a board. Our favourite was a poppy on a bent stalk blowing in the wind. It was his special party piece.'

'Wait there, Gran,' I shouted. 'I'll go and get my picture of a poppy. It's my party piece, too!' I ran to my room, took the painting off my wall and dashed back to show her. 'What do you think of this?' I grinned.

I saw Gran lean forward to look more closely at her screen. 'Goodness, how did you get hold of that?' she asked.

'I drew it with charcoal then used a wash and watercolours,' I told her.

'That's amazing. Hold it still, let me look again. Yes, the shape and everything – even down to the bent stem and twisted leaf. That's exactly how Grandad drew it.'

I felt a tingle run down my back and told Gran how awesome it was. But, deep down, I was a bit unsettled. What did it all mean?

I found out just after our Skype session ended.

The little Bible was still on the red silk inside the case from the loft. I worked out both references and found the verses inside. The one in the New Testament had a small piece of paper tucked between the pages. It had another typed message on it:

4:1, 1:4, 1:16, 1:3, 2:9

2:9, 1:3, 1:16

2:2, 1:5, 1:16, 1:3, 3:3

2:1, 2:2, 2:3

2:14, 1:1, 1:1, 1:4

It didn't take me long to get the words but I didn't know what they meant. I thought about what Gran had told me. I read the two verses again and I put the Bible back in the case. As soon as I saw the colour of the silk lining, the message clicked. Something was hidden underneath – Moon!

I carefully pulled out the lining and saw a sheet of thick brown paper hidden under it – with all kinds of raised marks on it: *

---

* *Note:* the key is on page 99.

⊃ΓΛ\ Ր\Γ⊃⊃ᒧ

I <NO∩ ᒧOU LL NΓVΓ\ \ΓΛ⊃ −◦I/ ΛN⊃ I ⊃ON− /UᒐᒐO/Γ ΛNᒧONΓ ΓVΓ\ ∩ILL.. I JU/− NΓΓ⊃ −O ⊂ONՐΓ// −◦\ΓΓ ᒣO\Γ −◦INᒉ/..

Λ∵I LOVΓ⊃ ᒧOU\ ⊃ΛUᒉ◦−Γ\ Λ/ ᒣᒧ O∩N.. ⊃ΓΛ\ ΛLI⊂Γ ⊃IΓ⊃ ᒧΓ/−Γ\⊃Λᒧ. ΛᒉΓ⊃ Ր⊂.. I ΛL∩Λᒧ/ ᒣΓΛN− −O −ΓLL ◦Γ\ ΛLL ΛՆOU− ᒧOU ՆU− I NΓVΓ\ ⊃I⊃.. ՐO\ᒉIVΓ ᒣΓ.. ◦Γ\ LOVΓLᒧ NΛ−U\Γ ∩Λ/ JU/− LI<Γ ᒧOU\/.. /◦Γ ∩Λ/ ᒣᒧ LΛ/− LIN< −O ᒧOU ΛN⊃ I ՐΓΓL ⊃ΓVΛ/−Λ−Γ⊃.. /◦Γ NΓVΓ\ <NΓ∩ ΛՆOU− ◦Γ\ \ΓΛL ՐΛ−◦Γ\.. I ᒣ /O\\ᒧ..

Λ/ ՐO\ ᒧOU\ ՆΓLOVΓ⊃ ⊃ΛI/ᒧ.

I could never tell her either. I nursed her in her final years, but it seemed best to save her from the truth. I hope you understand.

While all seems silly now, but I felt bad about it for years. Do you remember the locket watch I gave you? I'm ashamed to say I stole it. It belonged to the squire, and he sacked one of the servants for taking it. You thought I'd spent a fortune on you. I'm sorry.

Why I didn't tell you the whole truth. Unlike you, I had a terrible temper. Now I know I am dying. I can admi-

I ƆIƆ ᒀᴧ\ ⅂O\Γ −oᴧN ⳑ∪/o −oΓ
/Γ\⅂ΓᴧN− IN−O −oΓ ⅂∪Ɔ −oᴧ−
NI⅂o−.. I −o∪⅂ⳑ ΓƆ oI⅂ oᴧ\Ɔ IN
−oΓ ᒀᴧⅭΓ.. I /oŌ∪⅃Ɔ N − oᴧ∨Γ
ƆoNΓ I−.. I ∩ᴧ/ ∩\o N⅂.. ⅃o∪
ⳑ ᴧIƆ −oΓ ⳑ\IⅭΓ ᒀo\ ⅂⅃
/−∪ⳑIƆI−⅃.. ∩oᴧ− ᴧ ⳑ\IⅭΓ.. I ᴧ⅂
/o /o\\⅃..

⅃o∪\ ΓᴧΓ\ LOVIN⅂ ᑌ\o−oΓ\.
⅂IⅬΓ/

JOoN ᴧΓ:ᴧⅭ
⅂\ΓᴧーΓ\ LOVΓ oᴧ−o NO ⅂ᴧN
−oᴧN −oI/ −oᴧ− oΓ Lᴧ⅃ ƆoᴧN
oI/ LIᒀΓ ᒀo\ oI/ ᑌ\o−oΓ\

I couldn't believe what I found clipped underneath that page of Moon. There were two faded but beautiful little paintings. One showed a skylark flying over a field with a tree behind, and the other was a poppy with a bowed head blowing in the wind. They were just like mine on the wall in my bedroom. But these, in my hands, were 100 years old. Written in pencil on the back was:

Giles – Happy Christmas
From Freddy – 1913

There was one more piece of paper with the paintings. It was a final typed message. Before I began to read it, I thought again about the painter of those pictures and I unbuttoned my shirt. I pulled the collar down over my left shoulder and there it was – as always. I'd never thought of my funny little red squiggle of a birthmark as an upside-down **f** before. But now, as I stared at it in the mirror, I saw it's a letter **t**. I now know what it means. I'm not only a twin, but a triplet.

Unless it's more than that. More than meets the eye.

It's a bit weird, but my birthday is directly linked to World War 1.

Surprisingly, I'm not a Gemini ('The Twin')

I wasn't born on Freddy's birthday, either.

Mine is in August. You can probably guess the date.

FREDERICK OVEL'S FINAL NOTE

I suppose we all have our secrets. There are many things we keep to ourselves – things we don't want to bother others about. I've always kept the past locked away and hidden – though seldom out of mind. My generation doesn't talk about a lot of things.

I've always boasted about being the same age as the century itself. But unlike the

century, I don't know how long I've got left.
Not long now. That's why I've written down
my full story for the family. Of course, I don't
suppose my confession will make much
difference to anyone ... but it will to me. I need
to set down what I've lived with all these
years. It's time to put the record straight.
Even so, it will have to wait until after my
death before anyone finds this part of the
record. I still can't admit to what I've done.

I was sent back from the war with no more
than a piece of paper stating 'UNFIT FOR
SERVICE – BLIND'. Because of 'the swap', I
was assumed to be Private Freddy Ovel – who
must have suffered delayed blinding after the
gas attack. I didn't tell anyone differently. As
far as everyone thought (apart from Gordon),
Giles Hoadley had been shot for cowardice –

with all the disgrace that brought.

I assumed that if I told the truth, I'd end up back in prison, or worse. The crime of being found guilty of cowardice was most shameful then. I was also full of guilt. After all, I was responsible for Freddy's death and I should have stopped them shooting him. Yes, I was in no mental state to think straight, so I went along with the lie that I was Freddy Ovel. It was easy to speak just like him.

They sent me to a country house in Suffolk, which had been turned into a military hospital. Most of us were blind or lame and learning how to cope. It was a struggle and many of us were in a bad way – but at least we'd come back alive.

I still had Freddy's last request to attend to, so I asked them to let Daisy know where I was. She came to see me shortly after giving birth to dear little baby Alice. We were both very emotional and I couldn't bring myself to tell her the truth. She was convinced I was Freddy and was overjoyed to see me. You have to remember she hadn't seen him for months and she'd been warned that, like all returning soldiers, he would be a different person. I still had facial injuries and wore dark glasses, but she even said I hadn't changed as much as she'd feared. She wanted us to get married quickly and secretly.

So yes, I married Daisy. I felt the Ovel family had suffered enough with Harry's death, so if I filled Freddy's shoes, not only would I save everyone's pain but I could become the twin I'd always wanted to be. Maybe you think I was deceitful and dishonest. I guess I was – but you have to remember the absolute shame of being told her beloved had been executed.

People could be very cruel to such families. So I did as Freddy asked and I looked after Daisy and little Alice, loving them as my own. Eventually we had a baby ourselves when Peter was born, and we lived happily for many years. We ran a successful business together – a sweet shop and tobacconist next to a cinema (till the next war came).

Only Gordon knew the truth and, even if the flu epidemic hadn't so cruelly claimed him after his return, he would have said nothing, I'm sure. His was such a gentle innocence – and yet he was one of the lions ... lions led by donkeys.

My sister Maud would probably have discovered the truth if she hadn't had enough worries of her own. During the war she was struck down with polio and was too ill to notice any marked change in her younger brother. She spent the rest of her life in much pain and needing crutches to walk.

I never met the Squire or his wife again. They apparently referred to Giles Hoadley as 'that terrible cowardly wretch who ran away to the war and got his just deserts.' They were even heard to say that it was most inconvenient as they had to rewrite their will.

I could live with that.

As for Ma, dear Ma ... I think she knew the truth all along. In her final illness, I sat by her bed and spoke softly into her ear, uncertain if she could hear me. She opened her eyes, squeezed my hand and whispered, 'A mother knows her sons.'

There is no mention of either Frederick Ovel or Giles Hoadley on any memorial or plaque. It's as if anyone executed (Freddy was far from alone) never existed. The awful truth is, had I joined up as 'son of the Squire', I would have been enlisted as an officer and

Freddy would still be alive. That is my everlasting guilt and why I've lived as a fraud to this day. You have to realise that, in my lifetime, revealing these secrets would still cause a scandal and be too much to bear for my family. But, most of all, bearing the name of my heroic brother has given me strength to go on. You see, mine had been such a sterile childhood, while Freddy's was rooted in the fertile earth of family love – the richest soil of all. And that's where I've always wanted to belong, too.

Freddy was a remarkable person. He had little education, yet he was wiser, kinder and more gifted than I shall ever be. Had he lived, who knows what he would have achieved?

Today I was taken to the cottage again where we were born. From there I walked along the brook to what used to be the hay meadow where Freddy and I once played. I stood very quietly on the hill, a breeze sighing among the poppies, and I listened to the distant song of a skylark as I spoke to Freddy again – all about another world ... far beyond the fields.

APPENDIX 1:
THE MOON ALPHABET

∧ A	∪ B	⊂ C	⊃ D	⌐ E	⌒ F
⌒ G	° H	I I	J J	< K	L L
⌐ M	N N	O O	⟨ P	⟨ Q	\ R
/ S	— T	∪ U	V V	∩ W	> X
		⌐ Y	Z Z		
∧ 1	∪ 2	⊂ 3	⊃ 4	⌐ 5	⌒ 6
	⌒ 7	° 8	I 9	J 0	

99

APPENDIX 2:
HIDDEN TRUTHS
AND LIES

In World War 1 (1914 - 1918) over 300 British and Commonwealth soldiers were accused of cowardice, desertion or even falling asleep at their posts – and were executed by their own firing squads. Some were only in their teens.

In 2006, the British Parliament finally granted pardons to WW1 executed soldiers.

'I hope that pardoning these men will finally remove the stigma with which their families have lived for years.' (Des Browne, the UK Defence Secretary in 2006.)

Many of their names did not appear on official war memorials.

The **Shot at Dawn** campaign claimed that executed soldiers were blameless because severe trauma and shock, not cowardice, had affected them so badly. Rushed court martial trials often used doubtful evidence and gave no representation for the distressed accused.

Opposite: The Shot at Dawn memorial to executed soldiers at the National Memorial Arboretum, Lichfield in the UK.

The memorial is based on 17-year-old Private Herbert Burden, who lied about his age to enlist and was shot by firing squad at Ypres in 1915.

AUTHOR'S NOTE

As a child, I stood with my grandad and other World War One veterans on a cold November morning at the cenotaph for the Festival of Remembrance. He remained very still throughout and, as I looked up into his unseeing eyes, I could tell they hid such powerful memories and emotions. Maybe he was also thinking of his baby sister killed by a cricket ball or of Maud, his older sister cruelly disabled by polio ... as a brass band played

'O God our help in ages past, our hope for years to come,
Our shelter from the stormy blast and our eternal home.'

This book is dedicated to Sam, Tom, Ben & Esther – whose great great grandfather (my grandad) served as a young soldier in World War One. Many years later, with trusty guide dog at his side, he was an active fundraiser for Guide Dogs ... and a dab hand with his typewriter.

A FINAL THOUGHT

Scientists now understand a lot about how the characteristics of parents (such as having blond hair or being tall) can be inherited by their children. This happens as a result of *genes* being passed on from one generation to the next. Genes are found in the bodies of nearly all living things.

Genes, and genetics, can probably explain how Sam and Freddy look very similar – to the point of looking like twins (or, in this case, Sam, Freddy and Giles looking like triplets across time). It can also probably explain how Sam was such a good artist (like Freddy).

What genetics can't explain is how Sam's drawings looked exactly like Freddy's, even though they were drawn a hundred years apart. Genes can make you good at drawing – but they won't make you draw exactly the same pictures as your grandad.

Around 1800 a French scientist called *Jean-Baptiste Pierre Antoine de Monet, Chevalier de Lamarck* ('Lamarck' for short!) suggested that children inherited characteristics that their parents acquired during their (the parents') lifetime. So if your father worked out in the gym a lot and developed big muscles, you would 'inherit' big muscles too.

At the time that Lamarck was writing, nobody knew about genes, so this sounded as if it might be true. Now most scientists think that it isn't the case.

Is there anything else in science that might explain the fact that Sam drew exactly the same pictures as Freddy?

How and what we inherit from our ancestors (including their experiences and memories) is a fascinating area that scientists continue to explore. The subject of *epigenetics* is likely to lead biologists to many more discoveries about what parents pass on to their children and grandchildren.

Some scientists talk about *memes*. These are like genes – they are passed on from one generation to the next. But in fact memes are nothing more than ideas, or bits of ideas, that live in our minds – like a part of a nursery rhyme or a popular tune, or our memory of the smell of burnt toast. Babies are born and people die – but these memes seem to carry on forever, jumping from one person's mind to another.

Perhaps one meme that carries on with many of us is our collective memory of the horrors of the first world war.

The past is part of us all.

SECRETS OF THE MOON

Reading and writing secret messages was once impossible for blind people. In the early 1800s, Louis Braille of France invented a system for reading raised dots on a page by using the fingertips. Reading and writing using Braille has been used ever since by people unable to see a printed page.

Blinded soldiers returning from war were often

unable to learn or use Braille, particularly if their hands were damaged. Reading Braille needs very sensitive fingers.

Other ways of reading using touch were tried. Ordinary letters of the alphabet raised on the page need to be very large to be felt properly, which causes slow reading speeds and very bulky books.

In the 1840s, a blind Englishman called Dr William Moon invented another system of raised shapes. The letters are made up of lines and curves, similar to the printed alphabet. These shapes are rotated or reflected to create the 26 letters of the alphabet, with dots added for punctuation marks and numbers. The system is now just called *Moon*, after its inventor.

As the characters are fairly large and many resemble the normal printed alphabet, Moon has been particularly suitable for those who lose their sight later in life, or for people who may have a less keen sense of touch.

The UK-based charity RNIB (Royal National Institute of Blind People) has produced many materials written in Moon.

In case you struggled to decipher the message written in Moon font in the story, or if you want to check whether you worked it all out, the letter to Freddy said this:

Dear Freddy

I know you'll never read this and I don't suppose anyone ever will. I just need to confess three more things.

1. I loved your daughter as my own. Dear Alice died yesterday, aged 63. I always meant to tell her all about you but I never did. Forgive me. Her lovely nature was just like

yours. She was my last link to you and I feel devastated. She never knew about her real father. I'm sorry.

As for your beloved Daisy, I could never tell her either. I nursed her in her final years but it seemed best to save her from the truth. I hope you understand.

2. It all seems silly now but I felt bad about it for years. Do you remember the pocket watch I gave you? I'm ashamed to say I stole it. It belonged to the Squire and he sacked one of the servants for taking it. You thought I'd spent a fortune on you. I'm sorry.

3. I didn't tell you the whole truth. Unlike you, I had a terrible temper. Now I know I am dying, I can admit I did far more than push the sergeant into the mud that night. I thumped him hard in the face. I shouldn't

have done it. I was wrong. You paid the price for my stupidity. What a price. I am so sorry.

Your ever loving brother,
Giles

Greater love hath no man than this; that he lay down his life for his brother.

John 15:13

We shall remember

A play '*Beyond The Fields*' is based on this book.
Anyone interested in performing this should contact
the author via *www.johntownsend.co.uk*.

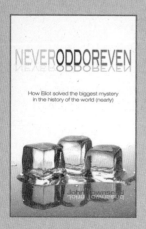

NEVER**ODDOREVEN**

How Eliot solved the biggest mystery in the history of the world (nearly)

John Townsend

Never Odd or Even

by John Townsend

'I'm at that special age: 12. It's one of my favourite numbers. 12 isn't just the sum of 10 (the base of our whole amazing number system) and 2 (the only even prime number in the universe) but it's the first number with 1, 2, 3 and 4 as factors. I reckon that's so cool.'

Here's a detective story with a difference. Eliot is twelve – and he thinks outside the box. He can't help it. Numbers are his thing – and letters. So when 'the biggest mystery that struck our school in the history of the world' needs to be solved, Eliot is the one to call on.

But this time the solution doesn't lie in the real world (or in the 'real' world of the story). Instead, the solution lies *inside the book* itself – only it's locked away in a series of puzzles and palindromes.

Can you spot the hidden clues and find the culprit?

Paupers

by Mary Chapman

'What kind of place is this, where families are kept apart and a simple act of kindness is punished?'

Lydia Maddison and her family have nowhere to go. Their father has left them – and left them with nothing.

So begins their time at the workhouse, as paupers, in Victorian England.

It's a hard way to live: families are separated, talking is forbidden and there is little food and plenty of hard work.

Lydia's son Tom and his sister Rose need to summon all their strength and ingenuity to survive – especially as Rose has a baby of her own to look after.

What does the future hold for the Maddison family?

Cold Fusion is a new series for readers who are curious, who enjoy a challenge and who like thinking outside the box.